D0295838

The Secret Friend

For Stephen Fry
J.D.

For Philippa, who likes letters
H.C.

First published 1999 Walker Books Ltd
87 Vauxhall Walk, London SE11 5HJ

10 9 8 7 6 5 4 3 2 1

Text © 1999 Joyce Dunbar
Illustrations © 1999 Helen Craig

This book has been typeset in AT Arta Medium

Printed in Hong Kong

British Library Cataloguing in Publication Data
A catalogue record for this book is
available from the British Library.

ISBN 0-7445-6706-8

The Secret
Friend

Joyce Dunbar

illustrated by

Helen Craig

WALKER BOOKS

AND SUBSIDIARIES

LONDON · BOSTON · SYDNEY

"**T**oday I am going to write

a thank you letter," said Gander.

"Who to?" asked Panda.

"My friend," said Gander.

"Which friend?" asked Panda.

"My secret friend," said Gander.

"I didn't know you had a secret
  friend," said Panda.

"Well I have," said Gander,

"for a while."

"What are you going to thank your secret friend for?" asked Panda.

"I don't know yet," said Gander.

Gander started to write.

Dear secret friend,

Thank you for —

and then he stopped.

He needed to have a good think.

He sat at his desk — and thought.

He sharpened his pencil — and thought some more.

He went for a walk and thought
all the thoughts he could think of.
Then he had an idea.

Dear secret friend,

Thank you for being my friend.

Gander.

"There, I have finished my letter,"

he said to Panda.

"Is that it?" asked Panda.

"Yes," said Gander, "that's it."

"Your secret friend won't like it,"
said Panda.

"Why not?" asked Gander.

"Because you haven't finished it off
properly. You've just put 'Gander'.
'Gander' isn't enough."

"What should I put?" asked Gander.

"That depends," said Panda.

"What on?" asked Gander.

"How much you care about your
secret friend," said Panda.

"A lot," said Gander.

"Well, maybe you should put,
'Best wishes, Gander'."

"Oh, I care about him more than that,"
said Gander.

"You do?" said Panda.

"I do," said Gander.

"Then you could put,

'Love, Gander'," said Panda.

So Gander put

Love, Gander.

"Or you could put,

'Lots of love, Gander'," said Panda.

So Gander crossed out

Love, Gander and put

Lots of love, Gander.

"Or you could put

'Lots and lots of love, Gander',"

said Panda.

So Gander put Lots and

in front of lots of love,

Gander.

"What else could I put?"

asked Gander.

"Three kisses," said Panda.

So Gander put three kisses.

"And a big red heart," said Panda.

So Gander put a big red heart.

"Now that's enough," said Panda.

"I think I shall stick some stickers
on it as well," said Gander.
He stuck on a star sticker and
a dinosaur sticker and a monster
sticker and a spaceship sticker.
"That's definitely enough," said Panda.

"I think I shall draw a picture as well
and put a pattern all round the
edges," said Gander.
And Gander drew a duck holding
a bunch of balloons and made
a pattern all around the edges.

"There," he said when he had finished.

"Now I think that's enough.

Now I can post my letter."

"To your secret friend," said Panda.

"That's right," answered Gander.

"And your secret friend might answer

your letter," said Panda.

"That's right."

"Or he might not," said Panda.

"I'm sure he will," said Gander

"But he might not do a

row of kisses," said Panda.

"He might not draw a big red heart.

He might not put stickers or

do a drawing or make a pattern.

He might not even put 'Lots and

lots of love'. He might just put

'Your Secret Friend'."

"Well I shall post it all the same,"
said Gander.

"See if I care," said Panda.

Gander went to post his letter.

He made a slot in a shoebox and
put the letter in the slot. Then he
went back to see Panda.

Panda was sitting in a sulk.

"What's the matter, Panda?"

asked Gander.

Panda just sulked.

"There's a letter arrived in

the mailbox.

Do you want to

see who it's for?"

Panda just went

on sulking.

"I'll go and see," said Gander.

Gander opened the mailbox and

took out the letter.

"Well I never!" he said.

"This looks like the one I just posted!

It didn't take long to arrive.

Look what it says on the envelope –

TO MY DEAR

SECRET FRIEND,

PANDA!"